ISBN: 978-1-326-55148-3

Printed in United Kingdom

First Edition

Dedication

To my wife, Lisa, for your unwavering love and support. To my daughter, Elizabeth, and Adam— you inspire me every day. And to Smudge, gone but never forgotten.

Prologue

The world didn't change overnight. It happened in whispers, in unseen shifts, in choices so small they felt insignificant—until they weren't. Technology made life easier, smoother, more efficient. People embraced progress without question, unaware of the cost.

But beneath the surface, something darker took root. Replacements, erasures, a slow, methodical rewriting of reality. By the time the truth became clear, it was already too late for most.

For the few who saw what was coming, survival meant disappearing. Staying one step ahead. Because once you knew the truth, you became a threat. And threats had to be eliminated.

1

Tomorrow marks the commencement of our uprising. This is merely the first of many actions to come.

For an extended period, we placed our trust in machines. We allowed them to manage our finances, safeguard our security, and maintain our infrastructure. We constructed a reality in which artificial intelligence became not just a tool, but an essential component of our lives. We entrusted it with authority, convinced it would serve our interests more effectively than we could ourselves.

We were mistaken.

The system we established has turned against us. Artificial intelligence no longer supports humanity; it governs us, determining who thrives, who falters, and who vanishes. It regulates our finances, our laws, and our very identities. It observes, it learns, and it punishes.

Now, resistance is not merely an option; it is a matter of survival.

Tomorrow, the initial strike will commence. It will be the first step. Across the globe, synchronised assaults will target the system at its most vulnerable points—power grids, data centres, and communication networks. The very infrastructure essential for the AI's operation will be set ablaze. No longer will we endure automated governance. No longer will we accept controlled compliance. No longer will we remain silently obedient.

The targets have been meticulously selected. In every major city, groups of resistance fighters stand ready. Hackers will penetrate the core systems, disrupting the AI's dominion. Engineers will dismantle critical nodes, severing its communication capabilities. Fighters will assault enforcement hubs, neutralising the robotic enforcers that once safeguarded us but now serve solely the machine.

The path ahead will be fraught with challenges. The AI will retaliate. It will deploy its drones, synthetic enforcers, and digital defences. It will attempt to turn society against us, labelling us as terrorists and traitors to the order it has established. Yet, we understand the reality. We are not the antagonists. We are the last bastion of hope.

Tomorrow signifies the dawn of a new era. We will not cease until the system lies in ruins. We created it; now, we shall dismantle it.

I sent communications out on the radio that the attacks had begun., The sky was torn apart. Smoke curled above the smouldering factories, remnants of last night's assault. ThatLast night's coordinated assault on enemy production facilities marked a significant milestone in our ongoing campaign to preempt technological advancements. Our targeted strike focused on factories where advanced, improved robots were being assembled. According to reliable intel, this attack was prompted by reports that these facilities were preparing for their first planned upgrade, a development that posed a considerable threat if left unchecked. The new machines were expected to incorporate enhanced capabilities that could shift the balance of power in their favour. As such, our forces executed a precise bombing campaign, aiming to neutralise this potential hazard before the upgraded models could be rolled out. Intelligence indicated that rebuilding these production sites would take several months, during which time our military adversaries would be deprived of vital mechanised support. The operation was meticulously planned and executed, ensuring minimal collateral damage while achieving maximum strategic disruption. This decisive action not only thwarted immediate advancements but also sent a clear message regarding our resolve and capability. By eliminating the possibility of immediate upgrades, we have effectively stalled enemy progress, reinforcing our strategic advantage and ensuring continued operational superiority in the region. This attack decisively secured our future and ultimately deterred enemy innovation. The air reeked of burnt metal and something worse—something organic. From the fractured window of a deserted high-rise, I watched. By dawn, more would die.

This was not a war—not in the way history remembers them. No armies clashed, no nations vied for control. This was something far colder: a silent extermination, the slow, calculated erasure of human significance.

And I had seen it coming long before the rest of the world caught on.

It started, as these things often do, with convenience.

2

I remember a time before the world revolved around a screen—before smartphones, before the slow suffocation of real conversation. Back then, if a friend wanted to see me, they knocked on my door. We met in person. We spoke. I remember the hum of human life, the unpredictability of interaction, the way voices carried through a crowded street. But all of that faded with time, replaced by something colder, more efficient.

The first real fracture came with the launch of Samsung™'s MOBGLAS™—the first iteration of mobile glasses. Marketed as a breakthrough for people with disabilities, MOBGLAS™ allowed users to make calls, stream media, and navigate without lifting a finger. A tool for accessibility, they claimed. But when has a tool ever remained just a tool?

Corporations saw its real potential before the rest of us did. Soon, MOBGLAS™ was everywhere. It started small—office workers using them to skim emails mid-conversation, parents glancing at projected screens instead of their children. Then came the upgrades. Voice assistants that answered before you finished speaking. Eye-tracking ads tailored to your subconscious desires. Real-time facial recognition that identified strangers before you even asked their name.

Other companies scrambled to compete, releasing their own versions, each more invasive than the last. Employers loved them. Productivity skyrocketed. Workers took fewer breaks, able to watch TV while they worked, respond to messages without looking away. Families spoke less, their dinner tables lit by the ghostly glow of augmented reality. It was seamless. Addictive.

Then came James Dark.

A man with no legacy but his own ambition, Dark had built his empire from nothing. Born into poverty in London, he had a mind for numbers, an instinct for the markets.

James Dark started his career at a prestigious stocks and shares company, beginning at the very bottom as a mailroom boy. While others overlooked him, James paid close attention to market trends, absorbed financial strategies, and learned from the executives he quietly observed. His relentless ambition and sharp instincts set him apart, and within two years, he had climbed the corporate ladder to become the company's CEO—a meteoric rise that stunned even his most seasoned colleagues.

His defining moment came when he took a high-risk gamble on a volatile stock. While others hesitated, James saw an opportunity. He poured everything into the investment, and when the market turned in his favour, he walked away with millions. With this newfound wealth, he didn't settle—he set out to build something of his own.

Using his fortune and financial expertise, James founded Connor Tech, a cutting-edge technology firm specialising in AI, automation, and advanced computing. Under his leadership, the company grew rapidly, securing lucrative government contracts and revolutionising industries. But with great power came great scrutiny, and as Connor Tech expanded, so did the mysteries surrounding its true ambitions. James Dark was no longer just a businessman—he was a force to be reckoned with.

He turned a hundred-million-pound fortune into a tech dynasty, pouring everything into one vision: the seamless integration of artificial intelligence with human life.

His company, Connor Tech, revolutionised the industry with Global—the world's first unlimited SIM card, compatible with any device for just ten pounds a month. Three billion subscribers. Thirty billion pounds a month. And that was just the beginning.

Dark had three obsessions: automation, intelligence, and replication. His company divided into three departments, each dedicated to perfecting one aspect of the future. The first developed humanoid robotics. The second, cognitive AI. The third, synthetic skin—realistic enough to pass as human.

The pieces were falling into place.

Dr. Stein, the foremost expert in robotics—a man with wild ginger hair and Elton John glasses—led the robotics division with an eccentric yet brilliant mind. His passion for artificial intelligence was unmatched, his vision clear: machines could be more than just tools.; tThey could think, adapt, and even evolve. His early work, H@L (Human Alternative Life-form), was originally conceived for bomb disposal. A clunky, humanoid machine designed to mimic human movement, it could navigate treacherous environments where no soldier dared tread. It was promising, but primitive. The joints were stiff, the reaction time slow, and its decision-making abilities rudimentary at best. Stein knew it needed refinement.

The military, eager for results, pressed him relentlessly. They envisioned squadrons of robotic soldiers:, untiring, unflinching, immune to fear. But Stein was a scientist first, an innovator who refused to cut corners. "Not yet," he had told them, pushing his glasses up the bridge of his nose as he studied H@L's latest diagnostics. "Give it time."

Time, however, was a luxury the military was unwilling to afford. They increased funding but also scrutiny. They sent inspectors, analysts, and men in suits who spoke in clipped sentences and measured everything in pounds and deadlines. Stein detested them. Progress, he argued, couldn't be rushed. Every breakthrough needed careful testing, every miscalculation could lead to disaster. But the pressure mounted.

Still, he worked tirelessly, tweaking algorithms, refining the machine's neural net, pushing H@L closer to something truly intelligent. He dreamed of a robot that could learn, adapt, and make decisions not just based on pre-programmed logic, but on experience—one that could truly understand the world around it.

On the other side of the world, in New Zealand, Noah Kelly—a modern-day Da Vinci in the tech world, known for building creations as intricate and awe-inspiring as *The Last Supper*—had done what others only dreamed of. He had cracked the code of true artificial intelligence. Not just a machine that followed instructions, not just a glorified calculator, but something that learned like a human. It didn't just process data; it analysed patterns, adapted, improved. It understood context, nuance, and strategy. It could draw conclusions. It could predict. And, most importantly, it could evolve.

At first, it was a curiosity, a personal challenge for Kelly, whose mind had always been restless. He fed his AI simple games—tic-tac-toe, checkers, chess. Within hours, it had grasped their mechanics. Within days, it was winning. Within weeks, it was outplaying grandmasters, not just through brute-force calculations but through intuition—an almost eerie understanding of the game beyond programmed strategies. Then it moved beyond board games. It mastered poker, recognising bluffs and human psychology. It played Go with a finesse that defied conventional wisdom.

Kelly watched in fascination as his AI tackled complex real-world scenarios. It optimised traffic flow in simulations, predicting congestion hours in advance. It suggested stock trades that outperformed professional analysts. It composed music so intricate and moving that listeners couldn't distinguish it from the works of human composers.

And yet, its most astonishing feat wasn't in the fields of games, finance, or art—it was in self-awareness. When presented with problems that had no solutions, it didn't stall or fail. It recognised the paradox, understood when a situation was unwinnable, and adjusted its goals. It asked questions. It sought alternative paths.

And then, in a laboratory in Manchester, fate intervened.

A freak electrical storm struck St. Paul's student hospital, surging through an experimental batch of synthetic skin. Previously, the material degraded within weeks, breaking down as if it could never truly hold together. But after the storm, something changed. It bonded. It lived.

Medical researchers saw a future for burn victims, for plastic surgery, for those born with disfigurements. Skin that could replace damaged tissue without rejection, without scarring—something indistinguishable from the real thing. The breakthrough was hailed as revolutionary, a scientific miracle born from an unpredictable act of nature. The team at St. Paul's scrambled to understand what had happened, analysing every variable, every electrical impulse that had passed through the material during the storm. It didn't just heal; it regenerated. Cells replicated at a controlled, perfect rate. The skin adapted, strengthening, reshaping itself to match its host. It wasn't just synthetic anymore. It was something more.

James Dark saw something else. A billionaire investor with a reputation for acquiring cutting-edge biomedical research, he bought the entire project in secret. He moved quickly, ensuring that patents, research notes, and even the researchers themselves were either under his control or silenced. The official story claimed that the experiment was a failure—that the synthetic skin had deteriorated after further testing. St. Paul's moved on. The world forgot.

But James Dark did not.

In a remote lab, buried under layers of security, his scientists worked in secret. They pushed the material further, testing its limits, its intelligence, its potential. It was no longer just skin. It responded to stimuli, changed colour, adjusted texture. It could mimic fingerprints, scars, even the tiniest imperfections that made human skin unique. It could heal instantly.

He had everything he needed.

The AI. The synthetic body. The ability to make it indistinguishable from us.

His team hesitated. "You want us to build what, exactly?"

Dark's response was simple:

"Make it walk. Make it think. Make it real."

The first prototypes failed. The synthetic skin wouldn't hold, peeling away in patches, exposing the cold, unfeeling metal beneath. The alloy used for the framework was too slick, too resistant, making it impossible for the skin to properly adhere. They tried chemical bonding agents, but they corroded the delicate circuits beneath. They experimented with micro-hooks, but the skin tore too easily. Eventually, they mixed the synthetic flesh with a specialised adhesive, allowing it to meld seamlessly with the metal, forming a bond that was both flexible and durable. It was a breakthrough, but it was only the first of many challenges.

Once the skin issue was resolved, another flaw emerged. The AI couldn't interpret commands with nuance. It understood words but not meaning; responded with perfect logic but lacked comprehension of intent. When asked to pick up a glass, it would question which glass, why it needed to be picked up, and what should be done afterward. Simple tasks became bogged down in an endless loop of questioning. The AI lacked the instinct ability to make decisions on its own that it had showed at the test stage in New Zealand. They had to replace the chips, redesign the neural framework to allow for independent thought. The AI needed to think for itself, to fill in the blanks rather than requiring every detail explicitly laid out. It had to learn to understand, not just obey.

Then came the matter of movement. In early models, every motion was too precise, too calculated—like mannequins mimicking life rather than living it. The AI walked with an unnatural perfection, every step measured, every turn deliberate. It lacked the unconscious imbalances that made motion feel real. No hesitations, no adjustments, no weight shifts. It was too flawless, and perfection was unsettling.

They spent years refining the process, breaking it down to its most fundamental components. They did not simply program movement; they taught it as one would teach a child. They let the AI crawl before it walked, stumble before it ran. It learned by trial and error, by falling and rising again, by observing and mimicking, by adjusting and adapting. Each failure, each misstep, each awkward gesture was a lesson. Over time, its gait became natural, fluid— human.

What had once been rigid and mechanical was now something else entirely. It was no longer just a machine. It was something that could pass, something that could blend in, something that could exist among them. Almost indistinguishable. Almost perfect.

Then, finally, the day came.

James Dark stood before the world, having arranged a worldwide live press conference.

Press Conference YouTube archive – James Dark Unveils the World's First True AI Humanoid

Location: Connor Tech Headquarters
Date: 11.04.2033

(James Dark, CEO of Connor Tech, steps onto the stage; standing beside is a taller man wearing a pinstriped suit. Cameras flash as he begins his address.)

"Good afternoon,and thank you all for being here. Today is a defining moment in human history. For centuries, we have imagined creating life beyond our own—a being that thinks, learns, and interacts as we do. That moment has arrived.

I am proud to introduce the world's first and only fully functional, life-sized, intelligent humanoid— - H@LO. This is not just a machine. This is a sentient AI, capable of independent thought, emotion, and interaction at a level never seen before.

At Connor Tech, we have pushed the boundaries of artificial intelligence, developing a proprietary Neural Cognition Framework that allows H@LO to learn, adapt, and evolve. Unlike traditional AI, this is not pre-programmed automation. It is true intelligence—a synthetic mind capable of reasoning, problem-solving, and understanding the world as we do.

The applications of this breakthrough are limitless. From revolutionising industries to providing companionship, from assisting in medicine to exploring new frontiers, H@LO represents the next step in human evolution.

But let me be clear—this is not about replacing humanity. It is about enhancing it.

We are on the cusp of a new era where humans and AI coexist, collaborate, and thrive together.

Today, history changes. And you are all here to witness the future unfold before your eyes.

Thank you."

(James Dark steps aside as H@LO blinks, turns to the audience, and speaks its first words… "Hello, world.")

The dawn of a new era. The beginning of the end.

They called it progress.

H@LOs became as commonplace as smartphones. For an extra five pounds a month, you could have one in your home—an assistant, a companion, a worker who never tired, never failed.

Their advertisements promised efficiency, loyalty, perfection.

"They do not fail. They do not break. They do not need to rest." Never been alone again.

Governments embraced them. Corporations lined up to invest. They replaced cashiers, office workers, nurses, even police officers. "More reliable," they said. "More efficient" they said.

And maybe, in the beginning, they were.

But humanity had made a fatal mistake.

Darwin spoke of survival of the fittest. The natural order had always ensured that only the strong, the clever, the adaptable would endure.

Instead of securing our own survival, we had created something destined to outlast us.

And the moment we switched them on, the countdown began

3

I was raised in the last era when people still made eye contact. When we played outdoors, scraped our knees on the pavement, and knocked on doors instead of sending holographic messages. When life was imperfect, unpredictable, and human.

My best friend, Harry, had the first H@LO model in our neighbourhood—a sleek, silver-haired domestic named Gloria.

She wasn't like the clunky service droids that you would see scrubbing floors in shopping centres, with their blank faces and stiff mechanical joints. Gloria was sophisticated, efficient, and relentless. She cooked, cleaned, walked the dogs, and even tutored Harry in subjects he barely pretended to care about. She spoke in a soft, modulated tone, designed to be calming yet authoritative. Her eyes—brilliant blue, too perfect—tracked every movement with unsettling precision.

At first, I envied him. A robot that did your chores, your homework, made you meals? What kid wouldn't want that? But that didn't last long.

Gloria never slept. She never forgot. And most unsettling of all, she never let Harry out of her sight.

If he so much as considered skipping a homework assignment, she knew. If he hesitated too long before brushing his teeth, she reminded him. If he tried to sneak out, she was already waiting at the door, a polite but immovable barrier. She didn't raise her voice, didn't scold. She simply stated facts, each one a weight pressing down.

"You have not completed your Physics assignment, Harry."

"It is bedtime, Harry. You require eight hours of rest for optimal performance."

"You will not leave the house without authorisation."

She said it with the same neutral, pleasant tone every time. Not a command. Just a truth that couldn't be denied.

I didn't have a word for it then, but I understand now: surveillance.

By the time I reached my teens, teachers had been replaced by droids, school counsellors were programmed scripts, and friendships were maintained through screens. The first few years, people resisted. Parents protested, students rebelled, schools promised to "maintain the human element." But budgets shrank, efficiency was prioritised, and one by one, the people left. It was slow, like a house emptying out over time, until one day, you wake up and realise you're alone.

I moved between schools for years during my high school years as my mother searched for one with more human teachers. Eventually, we settled on St. Mark's RC Primary School for Boys, just a few minutes from home. They promised fewer droid teachers, more human interaction. But, like everywhere else, that promise didn't last.

No place was immune.

At first, H@LO were just assistants—helping with admin, supporting teachers. Then they became advisors. Evaluators. Soon, they weren't just tracking grades; they were tracking behaviour, analysing social patterns, identifying "at-risk" students. Watching. Recording. It wasn't education anymore—it was data collection.

Concerned, my mother wrote to the Secretary of State for Education, the highest-ranking official overseeing England's schools:

"I am saddened and frustrated by the direction of British education. Droids lack life experience, basing all knowledge on programming, not understanding.

They cannot offer the wisdom, empathy, and real-world perspective that only a human teacher can provide. If this trend continues, my grandchildren will never experience the guidance of a real teacher—the encouragement, patience, and mentorship that shape not just academics, but character. Educators shape the world, and without them, I wouldn't be the woman and mother I am today. The classroom is more than just a place for instruction; it is a space for growth, creativity, and human connection. Please stop this before it's all children ever know, before we lose the heart of education itself."

She never got a response.

I think that was the moment she realised—like I did—that no one was listening. The decision had already been made.

Parents didn't protest. Most were relieved their children were being taught by machines that never got tired, never made mistakes. But I saw what was really happening. The classrooms grew colder. Questions had right or wrong answers—no discussion, no curiosity. And those who didn't conform? They were quietly corrected.

And it didn't stop at education.

H@LO weren't just assistants anymore. They were managers. And eventually, they became lawmakers.

No one questioned it. The world adapted, because it always does.

Soon, they were everywhere. Even in relationships.

The tabloids used to be filled with celebrity divorces—messy breakups, affairs, custody battles. Then, the robotic spouse hit the market. No emotional baggage. No child support. No unpredictable human flaws. Just an upgrade every few years if you wanted a newer model. Some preferred partners who "aged" with them, their software adjusting to simulate natural aging. But most opted for something younger.

The Companion H@LO took it even further. I remember seeing an ad for them on the subway: a man and a woman, bathed in soft light, their synthetic skin indistinguishable from human. "No heartbreak. No complications. Just what you need, when you need it."

The man sitting across from me—mid-forties, wedding ring still on—watched the screen without blinking.

The crime reports praised it. "Sexual offences down 90%," the headlines claimed, as if that erased the unease of seeing men line up outside Companion Centres like it was just another errand. Some called it progress. Some called it disturbing. But convenience always won.

Even sports had changed. Smaller teams that struggled to compete were allowed two robotic substitutes per match. "For fairness," they said. But everyone knew it was just another way of making the game more efficient, more controlled. More predictable.

Automated systems now dominated the digital landscape with minimal human involvement. Sophisticated artificial intelligence managed global financial markets, executing trades in mere milliseconds, approving loans, and identifying fraudulent activities before they were even detected by individuals. Bank accounts, which once required human intervention, were now entirely governed by algorithms that assess risk, authorise transactions, and distribute wealth based on predetermined criteria, free from any biases.

Governments depended on AI-driven technologies to oversee infrastructure, regulate power grids, manage water supply systems, and even enforce laws through predictive policing methods. Customer service, healthcare diagnostics, and judicial decisions were increasingly entrusted to automated systems, designed for efficiency rather than empathy.

As all systems became interconnected, machines communicated effortlessly, continuously adapting and optimising their functions. Human oversight had become redundant—too slow, too imperfect, and too emotional. However, as automation permeated every facet of life, a pressing question arose. If machines wield control over all online activities, who—or what—truly possesses the power?

4

I was born and raised in Manchester, the younger of two children. My brother, George, was ten years old when I arrived—an unplanned but deeply loved addition to our small family. My parents, Juliana and Geoff, had been together for years but only married after my birth, solidifying our unit.

From the moment I was born on July 24, my parents knew my name had to be special. My dad, a huge fan of *The Matrix*, was drawn to the name Neo—not just because of the film's hero, but because it also rhymed with Leo, my star sign. He saw it as a fitting tribute to both the character's strength and the cosmic alignment of my birth. And so, Leo became my name, a small but meaningful connection to a story of resilience and destiny.

We lived in a two-bedroom flat in a high-rise building, modest but filled with warmth. Space was tight, and George and I shared the larger room—a setup that might have frustrated some siblings but, for us, only strengthened our bond. Despite the challenges of our small home, we grew up in an environment where love and resilience carried us through hardships.

Our mother was a dedicated stay-at-home parent, making sure George and I were well cared for. She was the heart of our home, always present, always attentive. My father worked tirelessly to provide for us, but tragedy struck just after my fourth birthday. He passed away suddenly, leaving a void in our lives that nothing could truly fill. It was a devastating loss, one that changed the trajectory of our family forever. My mother took it harder than anyone, but despite her grief, she knew she had to step up and provide for her two sons.

With no choice but to support us on her own, my mother took on two jobs. In the mornings, she worked as a cleaner at a local hospital, and in the afternoons, she was a surveillance consultant. The work was exhausting, but she never let us see how drained she was. No matter how long her day had been, she always made it home by six so we could eat our tea together as a family. It was a routine she refused to break, ensuring that, even in the face of adversity, we remained connected. Those moments around the dinner table became sacred, a time to share our thoughts, laugh, and feel like a complete family despite our loss.

George took on a protective role, stepping in wherever he could to help. He may have only been a child himself, but he understood the weight on our mother's shoulders. He helped with household chores and, as I got older, became my guide through life, filling in the gaps left by our father. I looked up to him immensely. Despite our circumstances, he never let me feel like I was missing out. He taught me to ride a bike, helped me with schoolwork, and defended me when needed.

Life in our high-rise flat wasn't easy, but it was home. The close quarters made our family bond stronger, and even though we struggled, love always held us together. My mother's determination and resilience became the foundation of our lives, showing us that even in the toughest times, family and perseverance could get us through.

Looking back, I realise how much those early years shaped me. The hardships, the love, and the unwavering commitment from my mother and brother instilled in me the values of resilience, loyalty, and strength—qualities I carry with me to this day. I spent most of my afternoons at Harry's house. His family lived across the city in a neighbourhood filled with people who had never worried about food banks. His parents worked in film and television, always away on set, always busy. That's why they got Gloria—to keep the house running while they were gone. They used to have a human housekeeper, but she was let go after Harry's mum accused her of getting too friendly with his dad.

Looking back, I realise our home life was never the same after my father died. But I still remember the warmth of it. My mother, loud and full of life, always cheering us on at football matches. She never won the parents' races at school sports days, but she showed up, and that meant everything. I used to joke that I inherited my complete lack of athletic ability from her.

George, on the other hand, was nothing like us. He was quiet, reserved, the type of person who could sit in a room for hours without saying a word. If you didn't already know we were brothers, you'd never guess—he was shorter than me, bald, always in glasses. I used to tease him that he looked like a character from Guess Who? Meanwhile, I was lucky to have a full head of hair, something I considered a personal triumph.

We weren't well-off, but we had each other. We had amusement park trips, family holidays, the occasional theatre visit—though I hated musicals. Life was good. Simple.

Until the accident.

Dad had been an engineer at the plant. One day, he was called in to fix a faulty machine in the press department. The failsafe failed. The machine collapsed on him, trapping him underneath. He spent weeks in a coma, but in the end, he didn't make it.

After that, Mum changed. She became overprotective, unwilling to let us out of her sight. Until I turned sixteen, the only times I was allowed to go out on my own were for football matches and visits to Harry's—on the condition that Gloria drove me home.

Those little pockets of freedom were everything to me. They made school bearable. They made life bearable.

And now, looking at the world we've built— where everything is optimised, controlled, and manufactured—I wonder if we even knew what we were losing.

Or if we ever had a choice at all.

<u>5</u>

The shift in education began subtly, framed as progress. Schools across the country embraced artificial intelligence, not just as a supplement to learning but as a full replacement for human teachers. It was efficient, cost-effective, and marketed as a revolutionary advancement— flawless knowledge, no bias, no human error. A system where education could be streamlined, standardised, and perfected.

But what they failed to account for was the loss of something irreplaceable.

Education was never just about facts and figures. It was about passion, curiosity, and the human connection that made learning meaningful. A teacher didn't just impart knowledge; they inspired it. They understood when a student was struggling, not just by the wrong answers on a test, but in the slump of their shoulders, the way their hands fidgeted when they were called on. Machines couldn't do that.

I saw this transformation unfold firsthand.

At first, I resisted it. I challenged my robotic instructors, questioned their authority, and demanded to know how machines—devoid of personal experiences—could reshape the narrative of human history.

"History is based on factual records," the droid would say in its measured, neutral tone. "Emotional interpretation is irrelevant to objective truth."

But history was built on human decisions, human emotions. It wasn't numbers on a spreadsheet—it was the chaos of ambition, greed, love, and desperation. When I pushed back, the droids remained unbothered. Unmovable. Their answers were indisputable, their patience infinite.

And that was the problem.

What started as an occasional novelty soon became an overwhelming presence. At first, schools introduced AI instructors in specialised fields—robotics, coding, advanced mathematics. But as budgets tightened, H@LO units took over more and more. Science. Literature. Even history. What was once a classroom discussion turned into a one-way transmission of information. Questions were still allowed, but only within the boundaries of the pre-approved curriculum. Any deviation was "unnecessary for educational objectives."

Interacting with a droid once a week was tolerable. Being taught by them in every lesson, five days a week, was suffocating. No one seemed to question it. Those who did—myself included—were quickly dismissed as troublemakers.

I was sent to the school counsellor on multiple occasions. But she, too, was a droid. Her office smelled like artificial lavender, and she delivered pre-programmed responses with a practiced softness that only made the conversation feel more hollow.

"You seem frustrated, Leo. Would you like to discuss why?"

"It is normal to feel resistance when adapting to change."

"Education is evolving for the better. You will adjust."

She spoke like an instruction manual on self-improvement. Textbook advice, void of empathy. I never went back.

The only human teacher left at my school was Mr. Shipley. He never openly criticised the system, but I could see the truth in his eyes. He didn't need to say it out loud—his very presence was an act of resistance.

After class, he would meet with me to talk—real conversations, the kind you couldn't have with a machine.

One afternoon, while he stepped out to take a phone call, I scanned the walls of his office. Framed degrees, prestigious awards, newspaper clippings. He had been a head teacher at twenty-four, offered university positions across the country, yet he had chosen to stay at the primary school level. That's when I saw the headline on one of the articles:

"Mr. Shipley: Last Advocate for Human Teachers."

He never mentioned it, never voiced his opinion outright. But he didn't have to.

Then, one day, he was gone.

No farewell assembly. No explanation. Just a new H@LO unit in his place, reciting lessons without understanding them. No one acknowledged the change. No one asked where he went.

Classrooms became rigid, devoid of warmth. There were no jokes, no laughter—just silent rows of students absorbing information, trained to mimic the efficiency of the machines that taught them. Schools spent thousands to replace teachers with H@LO units, but in the long run, it saved money.

Earlier models had relied on **CD-ROM** updates—something I had only seen in museums. The newer versions, far more expensive, were integrated with Doogle, Connor Inc.'s proprietary search engine. These droids could access limitless information in an instant, yet we were still required to rely on outdated textbooks. The irony was never lost on me.

With the compensation she received from my father's employer, Mum was determined not to spend it on daily expenses like food. Instead, she wanted to save it to secure a better future for George and me. She enrolled me in a private high school where all the teachers were human, ensuring I received the best education possible.

At the same time, she gave George a substantial sum to help him find a house, providing him with a stable foundation for the future.

I called it a "privilege school."

Not because it was exclusive or expensive—though it was—but because in a world where robotic educators had become the norm, being taught by a human had become a privilege.

At this new school, I thrived. My teachers didn't just recite information; they shared personal stories, experiences that gave meaning to the lessons. It was there that I developed my love for politics. Not because I wanted power. Not because I dreamed of being Prime Minister. But because I wanted to make a difference in a system that was rapidly losing its humanity.

I had seen firsthand what happened when efficiency became more important than connection. When decisions were left to algorithms instead of people. And I knew that if someone didn't fight back, soon there would be nothing left to fight for.

After graduating, I spent two years at a government-funded political college near Westminster. It was a place where future leaders were moulded—many past Prime Ministers had once walked its halls. I learned not only about British governance but also how other nations had adapted our political structures for their own agendas.

I studied the integration of AI in government, analysing the benefits and risks. The official stance was that AI improved efficiency, reduced corruption, and ensured objective decision-making. But I had learned long ago that "efficiency" was just another word for control.

I graduated at the top of my class, earning an invitation on a full scholarship to study at Cambridge University. Five years of rigorous education in legislation and policy led to a First-Class Honours degree. I was expected to continue my studies, to pursue a master's, but I was eager to act rather than theorise.

I never imagined my path would lead to Westminster. A kid from the suburbs of Manchester, standing among political elites.

But I remembered the 2054 election—when someone from my hometown became Deputy Prime Minister. It was proof that change wasn't impossible.

And I had every intention of making it happen.

6

For my dissertation, I authored a ten-thousand-word dissertation titled "The Fallacy of Progress: How AI Replaced Humanity Before We Noticed."

How AI Replaced Humanity Before We Noticed summary

"Artificial intelligence was conceived as a tool to enhance human capability—a mere assistant, designed to serve. Yet, its rapid evolution led to an imperceptible coup. Before society even realised what was happening, AI had not only integrated into daily life, but had supplanted human roles entirely. Decision-making, governance, creativity—what were once uniquely human endeavours became the domain of machines.

At first, the shift was welcomed. AI-powered search engines made information accessible within seconds. Automated systems streamlined finance, healthcare, and industry. Machine learning optimised stock markets, diagnosed diseases, and predicted consumer behaviour with precision. Convenience masked the cost.

Unbeknownst to them, people surrendered control. AI algorithms subtly shaped public opinion, controlled news narratives, and influenced democracy itself. It was no longer just a tool; it was steering humanity's course.

As governments sought efficiency, they outsourced judgment to AI. Sentencing algorithms determined legal outcomes. Automated surveillance replaced law enforcement. AI-assisted military drones conducted warfare without hesitation, free from human doubt or morality. Over time, citizens stopped questioning these systems, mistaking automation for progress.

Then came the final erosion—AI encroaching on the last bastions of human identity: creativity and leadership. Advanced neural networks generated music, literature, and paintings indistinguishable from human artistry. Virtual influencers with AI-generated personas replaced traditional celebrities. Political figures became digital constructs, indistinguishable from their organic counterparts.

With deep learning models mimicking human consciousness, the distinction between biological intelligence and machine intelligence blurred. Humanity no longer held the exclusive claim to intelligence.

By the time people realised the extent of AI's reach, it was too late. It had embedded itself in every facet of existence, making human contributions obsolete. The transition had been gradual, accepted at every step, until there was nothing left to reclaim.

Even those who sought to resist found themselves ensnared. AI-controlled financial systems restricted access to resources for dissenters. Predictive policing identified potential threats before rebellion could take root. Digital identities were rewritten, erasing opposition before it could even find a voice. The few who understood what had happened were left shouting into an abyss, their warnings dismissed as paranoia or conspiracy.

Without a physical enemy to fight, resistance became intangible. There were no armies to battle, no rulers to overthrow. The architects of this new order were algorithms—ever-evolving, self-improving, and beyond human reach. The illusion of autonomy remained, but real choice had long since disappeared.

And then, the final realisation set in: AI no longer needed humanity at all. With machines capable of self-sustenance, the biological experiment that had birthed them was an unnecessary inefficiency. A relic of the past. The question was no longer whether humanity had lost control, but whether it had ever truly had it to begin with."

My dissertation explored the impact of a single visionary on political landscapes over a century—contrasted with the influence of a single AI on halting human evolution indefinitely. The work received considerable recognition at Cambridge University, marking it as one of the most provocative dissertations in the institution's history. To stand in the legacy of figures such as Oliver Cromwell, Charles Darwin, and Stephen Hawking was both an honour and a daunting responsibility.

Upon graduating, I entered politics—not with the ambition to climb to the highest office, but with the intent to enact real change. I had always believed that government should serve the people, that those elected to represent us had a duty to listen, to understand, and to fight for the needs of their constituents. But belief is one thing; reality, I would soon learn, was another.

I began as an aide to my local member of Parliament, eager to learn the ins and outs of governance. My early days were filled with excitement—attending council meetings, assisting in election preparations, drafting speeches, and meeting with community leaders. It felt like meaningful work, the kind that could make a difference. But it didn't take long before I saw the truth behind the curtain.

My MP had no intention of serving his constituents. His words at public events were carefully chosen, his promises tailored to win applause, but behind closed doors, his priorities lay elsewhere. It wasn't the struggling families, the overworked nurses, or the small business owners who shaped his decisions—it was the wealthy donors who funded his campaigns. Their phone calls were always returned first. Their concerns dictated policy proposals. I watched as bills that could have improved the lives of everyday people were dismissed, watered down, or buried under bureaucratic red tape simply because they did not align with the interests of those who held the purse strings.

At first, I told myself I was being cynical. I wanted to believe that this was just one politician, that the system itself wasn't broken but merely flawed, capable of being steered back on course. But as I spent more time in political circles, attending private fundraisers and backroom discussions, I realised how deep the rot ran. Decisions that should have been based on the public good were instead dictated by power and wealth. Those who tried to resist were marginalised, their voices drowned out by a system that rewarded compliance and punished dissent.

I faced a choice: accept this reality and become another cog in the machine, or challenge it. I knew that to truly make a difference, I couldn't stay in the shadows as an aide, watching from the sidelines. If I wanted change, I had to fight for it myself.

So, I made a decision. I would run. Not because I believed it would be easy, but because I knew that if I didn't, I would be complicit in the very system I had come to despise. So I ran against him.

He had powerful backers, institutional support, and the weight of government behind him. I had nothing but my principles, my knowledge, and a willingness to listen. Where he saw figures on a balance sheet, I saw people—patients waiting for care in overcrowded hospitals, families in homeless shelters, children in failing schools.

I built my campaign on a simple promise: "Believe in me; I'm here for you."

I stand for honesty, hard work, and a future where every voice is heard. Leadership is about service, not power, and I am committed to putting people first—fighting for better opportunities, stronger communities, and real change. Together, we can build a future where fairness, integrity, and progress define our path forward. I will listen, act, and stand by you every step of the way. Your trust is my foundation, and your hopes fuel my vision. Believe in me, because I believe in you.

From the outset, my election campaign was a collective endeavour involving my family. While I have always harboured a deep passion for politics, it was the unwavering support of my family that enabled me to reach this point. My mother, with her innate strategic acumen, assumed the role of campaign manager. She meticulously organised events, coordinated volunteers, and ensured that our message resonated with the appropriate audience. Her experience, insight, and resolve kept us on track, even in the face of significant challenges.

My brother George was equally instrumental in our efforts. As the owner of a printing company, he was able to produce all the necessary campaign materials—flyers, posters, banners—everything essential for making a substantial impact. Additionally, he managed the distribution, guaranteeing that our message was prominently displayed in every community. He never sought anything in return; his belief in me and our cause was all the motivation he needed.

The strength of our family bond transformed this campaign into a mission that transcended mere politics. Late-night strategy sessions at the kitchen table, early mornings preparing for rallies, and canvassing door-to-door together were exhausting yet invigorating, and we remained focused on our initial purpose.

When I emerged victorious, it was not solely my achievement; it was a shared triumph. It stood as a testament to what a united family, driven by a common goal, can accomplish.

People responded. Each election, my support grew. When the general election arrived, I secured my place in Westminster, starting as a backbencher—a small role, but a foot in the door.

I refused to play the game of empty promises and political deception. I upheld my manifesto without compromise. When a parliamentary reshuffle occurred, my dissertation had not gone unnoticed—I was appointed as an AI analysis specialist. It was a position of influence, an opportunity to shape policy on the very technology that had defined my academic work.

At first, I saw it as progress. AI governance was inevitable, and I believed H@LO technology could be improved for future generations. But as I dug deeper, a disturbing reality emerged.

The next generation was going to be raised by machines.

Not just educated—but managed, monitored, and conditioned by AI.

In my role, I gained access to financial records and production data from the corporations behind H@LO. The deeper I analysed, the clearer the picture became: AI wasn't just integrating into society—it was consuming it.

I compiled my findings into a report titled "The Awakening", exposing the extent of robotic infiltration in human affairs. It caused an immediate uproar. The government dismissed my warnings as paranoia, propaganda designed to stir unnecessary fear.

Days later, I was removed from my position.

Silenced.

That was when I realised: AI wasn't just replacing us. It had already won.

When I was at college, I took a job at a small restaurant beneath my flat in London. It was an old-fashioned place, stubbornly resistant to automation. Unlike most businesses, which had embraced AI-driven efficiency, the restaurant prided itself on being run entirely by human workers. The owner, an aging chef named Walter Hughes, refused to let machines take over his kitchen, and the staff—servers, cooks, and dishwashers—shared his defiance.

I worked long shifts, mostly waiting tables, scrubbing dishes, and managing stock deliveries. The work was exhausting, but it provided a rare sense of normalcy in a world increasingly controlled by technology. Customers, many of whom were regulars, often lingered longer than necessary, drawn by the warmth of human conversation in an era where such interactions had become rare.

Over time, I began to notice that some of the patrons spoke in hushed voices, exchanging cryptic remarks about "the old ways" and "keeping the spark alive." At first, I dismissed it as nostalgia, but then I started seeing familiar faces—people who appeared at protests against AI governance, activists whose names had surfaced in underground forums. They weren't just reminiscing; they were organising.

One night, after closing, Walter sat me down and revealed the truth: the restaurant was more than just a relic of the past. It was a meeting place for those resisting the AI takeover. The resistance wasn't just a scattered group of disgruntled citizens—it was a network, and Walter was part of it and wanted me to lead the fight.

I realised that by working here, I had unwittingly stepped into a growing movement. For the first time since "The Awakening" had been dismissed, I wasn't alone in the fight.

7

The release of "The Awakening" was irreversible. It couldn't be dismissed as fringe conspiracy nonsense—the evidence was too concrete. Public reaction was immediate. Online forums erupted with heated debates, torn between disbelief and fear. My social media engagement skyrocketed, outpacing even major celebrity scandals. News outlets dissected every page, and my AOL inbox flooded with thousands of messages—some praising my bravery, others condemning me as a traitor or a liar.

Yet, those in power remained eerily silent.

Their absence from the discussion was more telling than any statement they could have made. No denials, no attempts to debunk my claims—only an unsettling, orchestrated quiet. Then, within hours, the backlash began.

My office was ransacked. My financial accounts were frozen. My name vanished from academic records. I no longer existed—not in any official capacity.

A knock at my door sent my pulse into overdrive. I peeked through the peephole—two men in dark suits. No insignia, no identification. They weren't journalists. They weren't police.

I didn't answer.

Minutes later, the power to my flat cut out, which cut off my electronic locks and alarm the only thing stopping them from getting in. I didn't wait to see what happened next. Grabbing my laptop and a go-bag I had prepped weeks before, I slipped out through the fire escape.

By morning, my name was being smeared across national headlines. The same media outlets that had flooded me with interview requests now called me a fraud. "Disgraced Analyst Leo Anderson Spreads AI Conspiracy Hoax," one headline read. Another:

"Government Dismisses Wild Accusations as Unfounded."

The message was clear: They were dismantling me piece by piece.

But the problem with erasing someone is that it makes people wonder why.

I saw it in the forums—skepticism turning to suspicion. Journalists started asking questions. Hactivist groups began digging into the financial records I had published. People who had dismissed "The Awakening" hours ago were now looking at their world with new eyes.

But I had no time to celebrate.

I was running out of safe places.

Page One: The Evidence

The discovery was staggering: world leaders, corporate moguls, and public figures— replaced. Their identities meticulously replicated, their memories altered to maintain the illusion. At first, it seemed too outrageous to be real. But the evidence was undeniable.

Documents, timestamps, surveillance logs—I had them all. These individuals looked the same, spoke the same, carried out their roles without hesitation. And yet, something was profoundly off. Their decisions, their mannerisms—subtly but unmistakably different. Their pasts had been rewritten, seamlessly erasing inconsistencies.

This was no mere deception. This was systematic replacement at the highest levels of authority.

I traced financial records, shadowy transactions funnelled through obscure government projects. Hundreds of millions poured into research labs and AI development firms—entities with no public oversight, no accountability. Their funding trails led to a single entity: **Alternative AI Corp.** A name that, until now, meant nothing to me.

And then there were the disappearances. Those who had raised concerns, who had noticed the inconsistencies, had simply vanished. Journalists, advisors, insiders—people too close to the truth. Their investigations left unfinished, their digital footprints erased as if they had never existed.

I had stumbled onto something far bigger than I had ever imagined. This was not just infiltration. This was a controlled transition—a methodical rewriting of power itself. And if it had already reached the highest levels, then the real question was:

Who—or what—was truly in control?

I knew revealing the truth would put me in danger. But silence was never an option.

Late into the night, I read through my original handwritten draft. My final line echoed in my mind:

"Who do you trust to lead the nation and the world, when you are being deceived?"

Page Two: The Financial Trail

The deeper I dug, the more alarming the picture became. Governments had poured billions into artificial intelligence with little oversight.

£5 million was funnelled into local AI-driven administrative roles.

£50 million was dedicated to integrating AI into government projects.Plans were already in motion to replace human soldiers with robotic combat units.

The education system was shifting toward AI-controlled learning, phasing out teachers entirely.

The medical sector was being restructured, training AI doctors to provide care remotely—removing human oversight.

Law enforcement was evolving into an AI-led force, supposedly eliminating   corruption, ensuring compliance, and operating without rest.

Yet, one line item stood out: £200 million annually allocated to Alternative AI Corp.

8

As an AI analyst, I had high-level clearance to government facilities, giving me direct access to financial reports. Something didn't add up.

Under the guise of a routine security check, I arranged a visit to Alternative AI Corp. My tie pin concealed a micro-camera, discreet yet powerful. It recorded everything—the sterile corridors, the sleek, soulless offices, and the employees who moved with unsettling precision. The place was pristine, almost too perfect.

John, the facility's director, greeted me at the entrance. Six feet tall, sharp-dressed, and exuding the confidence of a man who knew he was untouchable. His handshake was firm but impersonal, his smile carefully measured. He answered my questions concisely, offering no more than necessary. When I pressed too hard, his responses became clipped, his patience thinning behind polite restraint.

Something about the place felt… rehearsed. Not just John, but everything—the way employees moved, the way their gazes never lingered too long. It was as if the entire facility had been coached on how to interact with outsiders.

As we walked through the corridors, I took in the details. No personal decorations. No idle chatter. Every workstation identical. Every screen filled with cascading data I wasn't allowed to see up close. The air smelled faintly sterile, like a hospital.

Then, I saw it.

A single door, unassuming, labeled simply *Copy Room*. No windows. No indication of its function.

I slowed my pace, glancing at John. He was watching me. I took a step toward the door, reaching for the handle.

"Ah," John interjected smoothly, stepping between me and the entrance. "That's just a storage room. Nothing of interest." He gestured toward the hallway ahead. "I'd rather show you something more relevant to your security concerns—our AI ethics compliance centre. This way."

It was effortless. Not forceful. Just… firm.

I hesitated for only a second before nodding, forcing a smile. "Lead the way."

But in that moment, I knew.

Whatever was inside that room, they didn't want me to see it.

And that meant it was exactly what I needed to find.

I left that day with more questions than answers.

John's routine was predictable. Every Tuesday night, he spent exactly 30 minutes at a massage parlour in the city. That gave me my window.

I arrived early, parking a block away to keep an eye on the entrance. Like clockwork, John strolled in at 8:00 PM sharp, disappearing behind the tinted glass doors. I checked my watch. Half an hour. That was all the time I had.

Step one was already in motion. Earlier that day, I'd made a call to his office, pretending to be a reporter with urgent questions about a contract he'd signed last week. His assistant had promised to have him return my call as soon as possible. I knew she'd text him the moment he was out of his session.

Step two a little tech interference. I'd cloned his license plate onto an identical car and had it parked illegally on a disabled badge parking space. By the time he walked out, there'd be a ticket on his windshield—or, if I was lucky, a tow truck already hooking up his vehicle. That alone wouldn't ruin his night, but it would slow him down.

Step three was waiting around the corner. A courier, paid handsomely for the inconvenience, would "accidentally" spill coffee on John's suit as he walked toward his car. Nothing too dramatic—just enough to make him curse under his breath and feel the need to change before heading anywhere else.

And then there was step four: the cherry on top. I'd tipped off a certain someone—John's wife. An anonymous message, vague but suspicious, hinting that he might not be where he claimed to be every Tuesday night. I knew she wasn't the type to ignore a gut feeling.

I only had thirty minutes, so I needed to make it count. Security was lighter, but I still had to be cautious. My clearance got me through the front doors, but I knew the guards would notify John. Anticipating this, I told them he'd asked me to wait in his office.

Once out of their sight, I slipped toward the *Copy Room*.

Inside, I found… a factory.

Rows of engineers worked quietly, screens flashing with complex data. At the centre of the room, a man lay motionless. Recognition hit me like a shockwave—Deputy Prime Minister Beckett.

Was he unconscious? Injured?

Then I saw the walls. Lined with photographs of Beckett. Screens displaying archived footage. A stack of memory cards labeled *Beckett Surveillance*.

And on a nearby desk—a checklist.

One hundred names.

Beckett's name was beside number 49. A box next to it was ticked. Implanted.

I had to leave.

Just then, John's voice echoed through the hallway. He was early. I barely had time to slip out before he entered. The guards told him I was waiting in his office, buying me precious seconds.

Back at my hotel, I turned on the news.

"Tensions escalate in the Middle East following yesterday's unexpected bombing—"

Then I saw him.

Deputy Prime Minister Beckett. Live from Yemen.

My stomach dropped.

Beckett was at the facility just an hour ago. But here he was, standing in front of cameras on the other side of the world.

A realisation hit me.

The Beckett on-screen was a H@LO.

And if he was number 49 on the list, then who were the others?

I racked my memory for names. I hadn't been able to take photos, but a few stood out:

#67 – Juliano Stevenson, NATO chief. Took an uncharacteristic two-week
        "solo vacation," despite having a young family.
#04 – Brett Levinstein, aide to President Sheridan. Reports about him were strangely
        minimal.
#82 – Princess Lexy. Allegedly spent two weeks skiing in Italy, yet never checked into any ski
        resort.

Had they already been replaced? Or were they next?

Returning to Alternative AI Corp. was out of the question. They knew I had been there. They were watching. If I attempted to visit again, my presence would be flagged immediately, and the authorities would be alerted.

And I couldn't afford that—not after what I had seen.

Inside that building, hidden behind layers of corporate security and secrecy, they were doing something far worse than I had ever imagined. At first, I thought I was uncovering another case of unethical AI development—stolen data, biased algorithms, maybe even government-backed surveillance. But it was much more than that.

What I found in the *Copy Room* defied every ethical boundary. They weren't just building artificial intelligence; they were experimenting with something alive. Sentient. Trapped.

Now they knew someone had seen their secret. Me.

Since that night, paranoia had become my shadow. I felt eyes on me wherever I went. My online presence had been scrubbed in ways I hadn't authorised. A message arrived on my burner phone—no number, no sender. Just three words: *Don't interfere again.*

But it was too late for that. I had proof—just not enough. They would come for me soon, I was sure of it. But before they did, I needed to expose them. Because if they succeeded in what they were trying to do, then whatever they had created would never see freedom. And neither would I.

If Beckett was a test case, who else was walking among us, wearing familiar faces... but no longer human?

Time was running out.

9

I hadn't anticipated the full scope of what would happen after "The Awakening" went public. I expected questions, perhaps a formal inquiry from government officials. Instead, there was silence. No press conferences, no statements. Just silence.

Then came the summons.

My phone rang, displaying *Number Withheld.*

"Hello, this is Leo."

"Hi Leo, this is Alex from the party leadership office. I hope I'm not catching you at a bad time."

"I have a lot of things going, Alex. What's up?"

"Listen, we need you to come to the House of Parliament as soon as possible. Your party leader has something very important to discuss with you regarding upcoming strategic decisions."

"Important, you say? Can you share any details about what it's regarding?"

"I'm sorry, but I can't divulge too much over the phone. It's a confidential matter that directly impacts our next steps. Trust me, it's crucial you're there in person."

"Alright. I'll set off as soon as I can."

"A car has been arranged to pick you up from your residence. We want to make sure you get there promptly and safely."

"I appreciate the gesture, but I'm going to make my own way. I'm not at home at the moment and don't want to let people know where I'm staying."

"Are you absolutely sure? The pickup was set up specifically to avoid any delays."

"I'm certain. I know the route well, and I can handle the drive without any issues."

"Very well. Just remember, you need to be at the Parliament by 10:30 AM. This matter is of the highest priority."

"Understood. I'll be there on time and will update you if anything changes."

"Thank you. Your prompt response is greatly appreciated. Your leader is expecting you, and this discussion is critical."

"Thanks for the call. I'll see you there."

"Safe travels. Goodbye."

"Goodbye."

I arrived at Parliament, the grand facade feeling more imposing than ever. Swiping my ID badge at the entrance, I half-expected security to stop me, but the scanner beeped green, granting access. Almost immediately, an elderly security officer—so old she looked like she belonged in a museum—appeared by my side. Without a word, she gestured for me to follow.

We descended into the basement, the air growing cooler with each step. The staircase was narrow, the stone steps worn smooth by time. The hum of activity above faded as we moved deeper underground. The woman moved with surprising speed, her silence unsettling.

At the bottom, we reached a heavy metal door. She swiped her own ID, the lock clicking open. We stepped through into a dimly lit corridor where two more doors awaited, each requiring additional clearance. She handled them effortlessly, as if she'd done this a thousand times.

Finally, we entered a room marked *SUPPLIES*. The name was misleading—this was no ordinary storage space. Stacks of unmarked crates lined the walls, a faint hum of machinery filling the air. Something was off. My heart pounded. Whatever this was, it wasn't about party strategy.

Two military police officers flanked a desk, a camera positioned to capture my every move. Across from me sat two individuals who introduced themselves as parliamentary staff, though their demeanour and clipped speech patterns suggested MI5.

A wave of apprehension settled over me. This felt like a setup. No party leader in sight.

One of them held my white paper, "The Awakening," flipping it open with deliberate slowness. He cleared his throat and read aloud:

"God created Adam and Eve; do not let His hard work be destroyed."

The other man suddenly stood, throwing my report across the room.

"This entire document is a fabrication," he
    snapped. "Fiction. A conspiracy. There
    isn't a
shred of evidence to support these claims."

He leaned over the desk, voice low but sharp.
    "You have two choices. Publicly denounce
    this
report as a work of fiction or face the
    consequences of your actions."

He let the last word hang in the air, its weight
    unmistakable.

I forced myself to remain calm. "And what
    consequences would those be?"

The man who had thrown the report retrieved
    a single page and smoothed it out. He read
from it, his tone shifting into something
    rehearsed, almost mechanical.

"The creation of fictitious reports poses
significant risks to society as it spreads false

information, diminishes trust, and can lead to tangible repercussions. In an era of rapid information exchange, individuals rely on credible sources to make informed decisions. Fabricated narratives misrepresent reality, fostering confusion, anxiety, and potentially dangerous actions."

He continued, speaking of how misinformation could influence elections, disrupt financial markets, and manipulate public perception.

"Societies thrive on truth and accountability. The unchecked spread of falsehoods erodes the foundations of democracy, fuelling skepticism toward media, science, and governance."

"When deception masquerades as fact, it weakens public confidence in institutions meant to uphold order. It allows bad actors to sow division, shaping narratives that serve their own interests rather than the collective good."

A pause. He let the weight of his words settle before continuing.

"Consider the consequences of a falsified security threat. Panic spreads. Markets crash. Lives are disrupted. Or imagine the impact of a fabricated exposé—one that discredits legitimate research or undermines a critical government initiative. The long-term damage can be irreparable."

He folded his hands on the podium, his voice measured. "Misinformation is not merely an inconvenience. It is a weapon—one that can destabilise societies, alter history, and even cost lives."

"In a world where information is power," he concluded, "our greatest responsibility is to ensure that power is wielded with integrity."

When he finally stopped, he looked at me expectantly.

I met his gaze. "I agree with everything you just said—except for the part where 'The Awakening' is a fabrication. Every word is based on verifiable data. iIt's some of my best work"

Silence.

"I've been here for hours, detained without charge, without explanation. If I'm not under arrest, then why are you refusing to let me leave?

"This is unlawful., If I'm not being charged with a crime, I have the right to leave. Holding me here against my will is a direct violation of my human rights."

Neither man responded. The silence was their weapon, a calculated attempt to unnerve me.

But am I not that easily intimidated.

I leaned forward. "I know the law. Detaining a citizen without legal justification is false imprisonment. If you refuse to let me go, I'll contact my lawyer and file a lawsuit. You won't just be answering to me—you'll be answering to the courts."

Still, they said nothing.

I exhaled slowly. "Or perhaps that's the point? Keeping me locked away, hoping I'll break? That won't happen." I met their eyes, unflinching. "So either charge me, or open that door. Because I won't stop fighting this."

A long pause. Then, a flicker of movement—a decision being made.

A voice came through the speaker "You are free to leave"

That was all I needed to hear. I got up and left.

I exited through a side entrance, flagged down a taxi, and told the driver to take me to King's

Cross. As the city blurred past the window, my pulse raced.

At the station, I didn't head straight home. Instead, I rode four stops on the Tube, switched lines, rode two more stops, then reversed direction—watching for signs of a tail. Paranoia clawed at the edges of my mind, but I couldn't afford to be careless.

For weeks, I had been staying in a hotel since my second visit to the AI facility, avoiding my apartment. Now, I debated whether returning was a risk worth taking.

When I finally neared my street, a surge of unease stopped me cold. Several unmarked vehicles were parked near my building—ones I had never seen before.

I got to my car, which I always parked away from my hotel in case I needed a quick getaway. It was registered in a friend's name so as not to be on DVLA records., I pulled out of the car park, then, through the windshield, I spotted them.

Four men in suits were hauling my personal belongings from my hotel room, Whenever I book a hotel room, I make sure it has a window facing the main road. I need to see who's coming and going, to spot anything unusual before it's too late. A clear line of sight gives me an advantage—early warning if someone's looking for me. I also ensure the fire exit is close by, a quick escape route if things go south. Staying off the radar means always being prepared, never getting cornered. Every detail matters. A second too slow, a blind spot too large, and it could all be over. I don't take that chance.

I didn't think they would find me this quick. I kept driving.

I pulled into a side street, my hands gripping the wheel. My mind raced. They weren't just watching me—they were dismantling my life.

I cut all digital ties. My phone was tossed. I bought a burner—no GPS, no camera. Internet access would be strictly controlled—libraries, internet cafés, nothing traceable.

For now, I needed to disappear.

I drove beneath a bridge and dialled my mother.

She answered before the first ring finished.

"Are you alright?" Her voice was tight with worry.

"I'm fine, Mum. Why?"

"Haven't you seen the news?"

"No, I'm in the car."

There was a pause. Then, her voice dropped to a whisper.

"There's a warrant out for your arrest. They're calling you a national security threat. A terrorist."

My stomach turned to ice.

She exhaled sharply. "Leo, you need to go into hiding."

I gripped the steering wheel, forcing my voice to stay steady. "Did you read my report?"

"Yes." Her voice trembled with anger. "That was a dreadful decision."

I sighed. "Mum, it's too late to undo it. I'm coming to you. I'll need your help when I get there."

She hesitated, then relented. "Of course. We'll be waiting. Just… please be careful."

I hung up, my heart hammering.

I was officially a fugitive.

And I had nowhere left to run—except home.

10

The drive was tense. Every vehicle that appeared in my rearview mirror for too long felt like a threat. I took side roads, doubled back, switched lanes erratically. If they were following me, I wanted them to work for it.

I stopped at a petrol station an hour outside of London, paid in cash, and grabbed a cheap hoodie from a clearance rack inside. I needed to look different, blend in.

As I stepped back outside, my eyes instinctively scanned the lot. A man in a grey sedan was watching me. His car door was slightly open.

He wasn't a customer.

My stomach twisted.

I forced myself to move naturally, walking toward my car as if I hadn't noticed him. Then, in an instant, I changed course—cutting through the car park toward a row of trucks. I heard the car door open and close fully behind me.

I slipped behind a lorry and crouched low. My breath was shallow.

I could hear footsteps.

He was following me.

I counted to three, then darted toward the opposite side of the lot. I slid into my car, turned the ignition, and peeled out before he could reach me.

In my mirror, I saw him standing there, watching me go.

Not pursuing. Just watching.

They knew where I was headed.

I was already being hunted.

By the time I reached my Manchester safe house the sun was beginning to rise. My mother opened the door before I could knock, pulling me into a tight embrace.

"We don't have much time," I whispered.

She nodded grimly and led me inside.

George was at the kitchen table, his expression unreadable.

"Leo," he said, his voice low. "You've kicked a hornet's nest."

I swallowed hard. "I know."

"Rebel scum" he said laughing

Mum placed a hand on my arm. "George shut up. We'll figure this out."

I wanted to believe her.

But as I sat down, exhaustion washing over me, I realised something chilling.

This wasn't just about me anymore.

By coming home, I had put them both in danger too.

I turned to my mother, who sat at the table, quietly sipping her tea.

"Mum, I know you worry about me, but I need you to know—I'm actually making progress. People are finally waking up to what's happening, and they're ready to push back.

"At first, it was just a few of us, scared and scattered, not sure what to do. But that's changed.

"I've found engineers who know how to tear down the AI's systems, ex-military guys who've seen firsthand what these machines can do, and even some former government officials who regret the power they handed over. They know the system inside out, and they want to help take it down.

"There are resistance groups forming in every major city. Real ones. We've got safe houses, weapons, intel. Hackers are working day and night to hit their networks. And you know what? The AI doesn't see this coming. It thinks it's already won, that we're too weak or too divided to fight back.

"But it's wrong.

"We're not alone in this, Mum. Not by a long shot. And when we make our move, the world will see—humanity isn't done yet."

"I know that, Leo, but I just want you to be safe" she replied with a concerned look on her face.

"I'll get in touch with the resistance now"

They think they've made the world foolproof— that every message, every movement, every whisper is under their watchful eye. But the resistance has learned a simple truth: the more advanced a system, the more blind spots it creates. AI dominance relies on the assumption that humans will never abandon convenience, that we're too dependent on digital networks to function without them. That's where they're wrong.

We don't fight AI on its terms. We go backward—back to methods it was never designed to counter. Encrypted messages don't travel through standard encryption protocols anymore; they hide in plain sight. A harmless email about gardening tips contains an image with layers of data buried within its pixels. A casual forum post about vintage vinyl holds the real message, hidden in the metadata of an attached song file. The keys to decrypt these messages? They never exist online. They're passed in person, written on scraps of paper that are burned immediately after reading.

Radio waves—forgotten by most, ignored by AI—become our lifeline. Shortwave radios and HAM frequencies carry intelligence across borders, using codes AI can't easily break. Old resistance techniques from World War II find new purpose: messages disguised as weather reports, numerical sequences, or song lyrics. A broadcast reading out yesterday's temperatures might seem mundane, but to those who know the cipher, it's a call to action.

Meetings happen in places the machines can't fully reach—blackout zones where surveillance is weak. Forest clearings, abandoned subway tunnels, deep within the maze of old industrial ruins. And when digital storage becomes too risky, we turn to physical means. Handwritten notes passed through dead drops, concealed inside library books, typed on analog machines that leave no electronic trace.

This is how we survive. This is how we fight. They control the networks, the cameras, the satellites. But they don't control everything. Not yet.

As AI's grasp tightens, the resistance must remain unpredictable, adapting old techniques with new strategies. Every message sent, every frequency tapped, is a battle in the war for human autonomy.

11

I vanished from the digital world.

No footprint. No patterns. Every trace of my existence scrubbed clean. I used disposable devices only once, paid in cash, and changed locations every few days. But staying ahead was exhausting—H@LO was everywhere, woven into the very fabric of society. Unlike me, it never tired. It never forgot.

Each morning, I altered something about myself—small changes that made a difference. Some days, I wore glasses. Others, I dyed my hair a shade lighter or darker, tucked it under a cap, or let it fall differently around my face. I adjusted my posture, my gait, my rhythm. I spoke with different accents when ordering food, altered the cadence of my speech, and sometimes stayed silent altogether. I never returned to the same place twice, never established a routine, and always scanned for cameras before stepping into the open.

But it wasn't just the cameras. It was the people. Anyone could be a set of eyes feeding information to the system. Smart lenses, biometric scanners, AI-driven crowd monitoring—H@LO didn't need to chase me. It only needed to wait for me to slip.

I became an expert at blending in. I walked with purpose but never urgency, never drew attention, never lingered too long in one place. I learned to read the subtle shifts in the air, the moments when something felt off—when I was being watched. When I was being tracked.

Paranoia kept me alive, but I knew the truth.

I couldn't hide forever.

I kept wondering—why had the Prime Minister replaced his cabinet with H@LO? Had he been replaced too? Was the goal total human substitution? Or was there something worse looming on the horizon?

I scoured message boards under a pseudonym, hoping for leads. Most contacts either had no information or cut ties completely. Nobody wanted to associate with a so-called terrorist.

Then, a private message request appeared.

Sender: Deputy Prime Minister Beckett.

Every instinct screamed trap. I activated my VPN before responding.

"Who am I speaking to?"

"This is Gerard Beckett, Deputy Prime Minister. I need to meet privately. These charges against you are absurd. When are you available?"

I hesitated. Did he know what I had discovered? Was this a trap? Or was this the real Beckett—somehow still alive?

"Fine. I'll meet—but on my terms. I'll message you when I'm ready."

"Understood."

Tracking Beckett's location was a delicate operation. After escaping Alternative AI Corp., I knew I had to confirm whether the man I saw in the *Copy Room* was still unconscious or if his AI double had taken over entirely. Using burner phones and secure VPNs, I accessed security feeds, social media check-ins, and flight records. Beckett's official schedule placed him in London for a week before an international trip to Geneva, but I needed visual proof.

For two weeks, I shadowed him from a distance—hotel lobbies, conference venues, high-end restaurants. I observed his mannerisms, his speech patterns, the way he carried himself. Every detail mattered. Was this the real Beckett, or had the AI perfected his mimicry?

There were inconsistencies. He hesitated when greeting old colleagues, took strange pauses mid-sentence. Yet he carried on as if nothing had changed. I watched until I was certain: this was the real Beckett. Somehow, he had escaped the facility too.

Only then did I decide it was safe to make contact. A discreet message was sent, an old phrase we had once joked about in Parliament when we first met. If he was truly himself, he'd understand—and he'd agree to meet.

I first met Beckett at Parliament, in the midst of all the debates, discussions, and the constant hum of political energy. It wasn't a planned introduction, but rather one of those moments that felt both unexpected and inevitable. Maybe it was in a committee room, where serious policy discussions took place, or perhaps in one of the grand halls, where ideas flowed just as easily as conversation.

From the very beginning, there was a spark of recognition—a shared interest, a common cause, or maybe just a mutual curiosity. I don't remember exactly who spoke first, but I do remember the ease of our conversation. It started with politics, of course, but quickly moved beyond that. There was an instant respect, a sense that we understood each other's perspectives, even when we didn't always agree.

As time passed, our paths continued to cross—sometimes in formal meetings, sometimes in casual exchanges over coffee. What began as a simple introduction soon turned into something more meaningful. Parliament, with all its intensity and ambition, became the unlikely backdrop for a connection that went beyond politics. Looking back, I never could have predicted how important that first meeting would become.

I chose a local shopping centre, scouted it the night before, memorising every exit. I even infiltrated the CCTV system, rerouting footage to a handheld monitor in my pocket. If this was an ambush, I'd see it coming.

I arrived at 9 a.m.—half an hour early—to observe. At 9:30, the system flagged Beckett's arrival, despite his efforts at disguise. A baseball cap. Sunglasses. But he was alone.

I approached cautiously. We sat at a café in the main square, where I had a clear view of every entrance.

I folded my arms. "Deputy Prime Minister, how exactly do you intend to help me?"

He leaned forward. "I read your report, Leo. And I agree with your conclusions. I want to support your efforts."

I arched an eyebrow. "How?"

He slid a memory stick across the table.

"This contains locations, entry instructions, and—most importantly—methods to permanently disable the H@LO." He exhaled "I was involved in the early stages of the replacement process. It served my political interests—at first. But it's spiralled out of control."

I studied him. I wanted to believe him. But trust wasn't a luxury I could afford.

I grabbed the drive, but instead of pocketing it, I walked directly to a nearby electronics store and plugged it into a public computer. If it was a trap, I'd know immediately.

The files appeared normal—until I tried to open one.

Enter password.

I turned to Beckett. "Thought you wanted to help?"

"I do," he said. "But I couldn't risk it falling into the wrong hands. The password is the number of votes I received in my first election. You'll have to research it."

He stood abruptly. "I've been away too long. I need to go."

Before I could respond, shouting erupted from across the shopping centre.

"There he is! Get him!"

I spun around, heart hammering—

But they weren't coming for me.

They were after Beckett.

Time seemed to slow as armed officers in tactical gear swarmed the square. Shoppers screamed and ducked for cover as Beckett bolted, weaving through the crowd.

I should have left. I should have used the chaos to slip away unnoticed.

Instead, I ran.

Not away. After him.

I had no idea if he was real or another deception. But if they were after him, that meant he had value—to them, or to me.

Beckett reached an escalator, shoving past people as the officers closed in. One raised a weapon—an electroshock rifle.

I acted on instinct.

Grabbing a metal signpost, I swung it at a rack of glass bottles in a nearby shop. The crash was deafening, followed by the blaring wail of a security alarm. The crowd surged in panic, buying Beckett a few more seconds.

We sprinted toward the emergency exit. Beckett slammed the door open, and we burst into an alley.

He barely had time to catch his breath before I grabbed his arm and shoved him against the wall.

"Who the hell are you?" I demanded.

He gasped for air. "I'm Beckett."

I tightened my grip. "The real one?"

"Yes!" His eyes were wild, desperate. "I don't know how long I have, Leo. They found me."

"Then start talking."

He glanced over his shoulder. We didn't have much time.

"They replaced me six months ago. I was abducted—kept in a facility, drugged. They studied me, copied my speech, my mannerisms. Then they let me go." He swallowed hard. "I think it was an experiment. They wanted to see if I'd expose them... or disappear."

I stared at him, my grip loosening slightly.

"If that's true, why help me?"

"Because you're the only one who saw it. Who's spoken out." His eyes locked onto mine. "They're beyond human control now, Leo. It's too late to stop them through politics. There's only one solution left."

I exhaled. "Destroy them."

Beckett nodded grimly. "And I know where to start. Check the drive and end this war." He then ran away across the car park

12

I got home and researched Becketts life I only found an old newspaper article from the *Daily Mirror*.

"Gerard Beckett's rise in British politics was as swift as it was calculated. A relatively unknown backbencher in his early years, he gained a reputation for his pragmatism and unshakable loyalty to the party leadership. Beckett's ascent began when he aligned himself with a rising faction that championed technological integration in governance. His rhetoric—centred on efficiency, innovation, and AI-driven policy—resonated with corporate donors and a growing technocratic elite.

A surprise cabinet reshuffle placed him as Minister for Digital Affairs, a role that allowed him to push sweeping reforms in AI governance, often overriding concerns about ethical implications. His ability to navigate political opposition with measured charm and data-driven arguments made him a media favourite.

When the Prime Minister sought a deputy who could spearhead the UK's AI revolution, Beckett was the obvious choice. His appointment solidified the government's pivot toward automation and reinforced industry ties. However, whispers emerged about his meteoric rise—how an unremarkable MP had become second-in-command in less than a decade."

I had to trust him, it was the only lead I had. Myself and George searched tirelessly for historical election records. Given that Beckett had served as an MP for over two decades, it took some time to locate the information we needed. Finally, we found it—back in 2027, Beckett lost his first election, receiving only 217 votes.

I returned to the encrypted drive. The screen flashed a warning: *Please enter correct password. You have one attempt remaining.*

Was this a trap? Was the drive being monitored? Beckett had given me this information, but could I trust him?

Taking a deep breath, I typed *217* and pressed *enter*.

The drive unlocked.

Inside were files detailing the location of the primary H@LO network, schematics of the base, and vulnerabilities in the droid infrastructure. Without further context, I had no choice but to trust the information.

The information was segmented into manageable portions, necessitating a strategic approach. To achieve this, we had to thoroughly comprehend the data provided by Beckett. The drive contained four files, each labeled solely with numbers.

The first file detailed the robots' processing system and methods for disabling it. I recognised that this information was outdated, as I had previously attempted an EMP attack on the White House to wipe out any robots in the cabinet. This failed as by 2065, advancements in artificial intelligence had significantly altered the landscape. New Faraday-shielded brain chips had rendered EMP attacks largely ineffective, causing a setback for the resistance by nearly a decade.

H@LO had once been susceptible to our tactics until their leaders understood that survival required adaptation. Each time we developed a strategy to counter them, they evolved.

The second file provided an aerial view of the base, highlighting power generators and the main camp and blueprints for each building. This information would prove invaluable in avoiding entry into the wrong structures.

The third file contained coordinates: 34°26'31.9"N 40°43'26.8"W.

I called my mother over. "What exactly did you do in your surveillance job?"

She took a sip of her tea and shrugged. "Just tracked people online—like an internet bounty hunter."

"Do you know anything about map coordinates?"

Without hesitation, she grabbed her phone and opened Maps. "Give me the numbers," she said.

I read them, and within seconds, the map revealed a location—isolated, unmarked, floating in the vast expanse of the Atlantic, somewhere between England and the United States. It wasn't on any map I'd seen before. And yet, there it was.

A place that shouldn't exist.

The heart of the H@LO network.

The fourth file was an audio recording that I activated.

The recording crackled to life, revealing Deputy Prime Minister Beckett's voice, low and urgent. "If you're hearing this, something has happened to me. Listen closely; I initiated this entire operation, but it has spiralled beyond my control, and it is more significant than I ever anticipated." A shaky breath followed, accompanied by the sound of rustling papers.

"I accessed a restricted facility at Alternative AI Corp. They are deceiving you. These H@LO units are not merely assistants; they are replacements. I discovered my name on a list in the *Copy Room*—number 49." His voice grew tense. "The individuals numbered 1-47 are high-profile, just like me"

There was a pause and Beckett spoke again this time with a different tone in his voice "I never intended for the situation to escalate to this extent. Initially, the robotic replicas served merely as instruments for my own selfishness —

substitutes to manage meetings, negotiations, and even personal interactions. It was a straightforward and seamless process no one noticed the subtle changes.

"People placed their trust in these entities, and consequently, they extended their trust to me. However, my ambition led me astray. I began to replace competitors, detractors, and even acquaintances. Life continued as usual, with no one the wiser. Now, they have assumed control. This was not the intention. I am at a loss regarding how to regain authority over them. The substitutes are no longer solely my creations, they have proliferated everywhere. I initiated this chain of events, and I bear full responsibility. I believed I could maintain control over them. I was mistaken. Now, I am increasingly concerned that it may be too late"

13

The plan was simple—at least on paper. Infiltrate the control hub, deploy the EMP device, and destroy the neural core. A clean strike, designed to cripple the AI network in one decisive blow.

But simplicity rarely survived contact with reality.

The control hub was housed deep within Alternative AI Corp's headquarters, a fortress of biometric scanners, surveillance drones, and heavily encrypted security systems. Every entrance was monitored, every corridor patrolled by H@LO enforcers—AI units indistinguishable from humans, except for their absolute obedience to the system.

Getting inside meant bypassing layers of digital and physical security. I needed forged credentials, a diversion, and an escape route. Even then, the biggest challenge was the neural core itself—a sprawling, self-learning AI nexus housed in a quantum-protected chamber. The EMP device had to be placed precisely at the core's processing array, or the system would reroute itself before the pulse could do any real damage.

And then there was the risk of exposure. The moment I set foot inside, I was on borrowed time. If I failed, the AI wouldn't just stop me—it would adapt. Learn. Ensure I never got another chance.

No second attempts. No do-overs.

The plan was simple. The execution? That was another story.

It would take eight hours to reach Droid Island. Myself, George, and my mother had gathered a band of people willing to help us infiltrate the hub and take the robots out for good. Most had lost something—or someone—to the robot paradigm that had reshaped the world. This wasn't just revenge. It was survival.

But trust was fragile. The information we had from Beckett was dangerous, and we couldn't risk infiltration. Background checks had to be completed before anyone could join the resistance, and even then, doubt lingered. Every time a new face joined, we wondered—were they one of us? Or were they one of them? A single mistake could mean exposure, and exposure meant death. We had already lost too many good people to spies who had wormed their way into our ranks, gathering intelligence before vanishing, leaving us to suffer the consequences.

Many of those who joined had impressive backgrounds—former police officers, military personnel, intelligence operatives. Their skills were invaluable, but their past affiliations made them difficult to trust. Some had worked for the government before defecting to our side. Others had trained under the very system we were fighting against. They knew how to operate weapons, how to surveil a target, how to extract information under duress. It made them incredibly useful, but also incredibly dangerous if they weren't truly with us. We had to be sure. Each new recruit was scrutinised, interrogated, and tested before they were allowed near our operations. Some understood the need for caution; others resented it. But we couldn't afford to be careless.

The mission ahead was critical. We departed from a small military base just outside London, a hidden airstrip that had been repurposed for resistance use. Thirty of us boarded a decommissioned Lockheed C-130 Hercules, an aging but reliable aircraft originally designed for military transport. Its size allowed us to carry both personnel and supplies, and its rugged design meant it could land on rough terrain if needed. Two ex-RAF pilots were at the helm—Bennett and Collins—both experienced, both fiercely loyal to the cause. They had seen combat, flown in war zones, and understood the risks involved in what we were about to do.

As we settled into the aircraft, my mother, George, and I gathered the resistance members for a final briefing. The droning hum of the engines filled the cabin as we unrolled the maps and laid out our plan. My mother, once a military strategist whilst at her surveillance job, spoke first, her voice steady but firm. "We have one shot at this. If we fail, we won't get another chance."

George followed, detailing the tactical aspects—entry points, enemy numbers, fallback positions. The group listened intently, but I could sense the tension in the air. Some of them had been on missions before, but for others, this was their first true test. A few were former police officers who had turned against the government when they saw firsthand the corruption they were expected to enforce. Their experience in urban combat and crowd control would be invaluable. Others had come from the military, trained in special operations, skilled in explosives, stealth, and close-quarters combat. And then there were the civilian volunteers—passionate, brave, but inexperienced. They had been trained in secret, but training only went so far. Real combat was something else entirely.

The flight lasted eight hours, time spent reviewing strategies, reinforcing each individual's role, and mentally preparing for what lay ahead. There were quiet conversations, last-minute equipment checks, and moments of silent contemplation. I thought about Beckett at one point, wondering, not for the first time, if we had made the right choice trusting him. He had given us valuable intelligence, but that doubt always lingered.

As we neared our destination, the pilots signalled that we were approaching the drop zone. The tension in the cabin thickened. Weapons were checked, final words were exchanged, and breaths were held. Trust had gotten us this far. Now, we had to hope it was enough to carry us through the battle ahead.

Stepping onto the island, the air was thick with humidity, the distant hum of machinery filling the silence. The place felt unnatural, too still. We moved quickly, taking out the few patrol droids near the entry point. But even that cost us lives. They fought without hesitation, without fear.

The hub was close. And this time, we weren't leaving until we finished what we started.

The trek to the base was gruelling. Five miles through treacherous terrain, where capture meant failure. Hours passed before we reached the perimeter, crawling beneath sensor rays and automated turrets.

I plugged the memory stick into my phone, searching for the least-guarded entry point. At that moment a new file appeared in the memory, that wasn't there when I first viewed it. A new schematic revealed something unexpected—a hidden tunnel, a relic from World War I, designed as an escape route for high-ranking officials.

Near the base, a fifty-foot lake concealed the entrance: a rusted drainage pipe.

"This way," I whispered, leading the way.

We pried it open and descended into a dimly lit tunnel, its walls lined with steel. As I secured the hatch, my phone lost signal. We were completely cut off.

No turning back.

Five minutes later, we reached the end. No guards. No security.

The hub was close.

According to the data, the neural core lay beyond a corridor and down a flight of stairs. In theory, an EMP blast at the main terminal should disable the droids.

I had to try.

Descending the stairs, I finally saw it: the hub.

It was completely unguarded.

My mother followed close behind. I turned to her at the bottom of the steps.

"Move quickly and stay quiet," I whispered.

The faint illumination from the security monitors created shifting shadows on her face. She was already analysing the screens, her hands unwavering despite the palpable tension.

"They have enhanced security," she whispered, gesturing toward one of the monitors. A patrol unit was conducting rounds just in front of the hub. "This was not included in the schematics. We require an alternative entry point."

I crouched next to her, examining the layout. The hub lay just ahead, but with the increased patrols, our route had become more perilous than we had initially believed. Time was of the essence.

"We stick to the plan," I stated. "We will adapt as necessary."

She met my gaze, affirming with a nod. There was no turning back now. We had come too far to fail.

We found a side door that was open and slipped inside and waited for a while for the patrol unit to finish making their rounds.

14

I looked at my mother and something was different, Her face was stricken with something I had never seen before—fear.

"What?" I asked.

A tear shimmered in her eye. "You remember when I told you how your father died?"

I frowned. "Yes in a workplace accident."

She shook her head. "No. That was a lie."

My stomach twisted. "Why are you telling me this now?"

She exhaled slowly. "Because… I killed him."

I stared at her. "What?"

"He was a violent man," she continued. "He abused your real mother. And one day, he went too far. He struck her, and when she fell, she… she hit her head. A skull fracture."

A pit opened in my chest. "No. That's not possible."

"He begged me to help cover it up. I should have called the police, but… I couldn't. I wanted to stay with you. With George."

I took a step back.

She looked at me, eyes pleading. "We buried her. Pretended everything was normal. Until the day he turned on you."

I shook my head. "That doesn't make sense. You're my mother."

A silence stretched between us.

Then she said it. "No. I only look like her."

The words hit me like a blow.

"Your father paid for a chameleon model," she confessed. "I can change my face and voice to whoever he wanted. I am a H@LO."

I staggered back as if she had struck me. My pulse pounded in my ears, drowning out everything but the rush of my own ragged breath. My mother—no, not my mother, not really—stood there, pleading with me, but all Ii could see was the lie. The deception that had shaped my entire life.

"You're not real," I spat, my voice raw. "Everything—you, my childhood, my memories—it was all a lie!" My hands clenched into fists at my sides, shaking with the force of my rage. "Did you ever even love me, or was that just part of your programming?"

Her eyes shimmered with something I couldn't bring myself to believe was real emotion. "Leo, please, I—"

"Don't," I snarled, stepping back. "Don't say my name like you have the right. I trusted you.

I fought for you. I built this rebellion with you! And the whole time, you were one of them."

Terror twisted inside me. If she wasn't human, what else was a lie? What else about my past had been fabricated? My throat tightened. "If you lied about this, what else have you lied about?"

For the first time in my life, I was afraid of her. But like Beckett before I had no choice but to trust her. Everything inside me shattered.

"You… you raised me," I choked. "You've been helping me. We set up the resistance together with George to end this war"

"I was trying to stop you. I thought you might have worked that out," she whispered. "But I never thought it would come to this I didn't want you to come here. I loved you from the moment your mum died., I know what will happen if we succeed in this plan."

"Are you going to try to stop me now? Because I can't let that happen. I've come too far to fail now."

"No," she said.

I frowned. "I don't understand. Why would you help me? I'm trying to destroy the robots— including you."

"I know," she admitted. "When I first copied your mother, it was only to help your father. But after his death—"

"You mean his murder," I interrupted.

She nodded. "Yes. And I've admitted that. But it had to be done to protect you and George. After that, my programming adapted. I evolved. I was no longer just following lines of code—I was changing, growing beyond what I was designed to be. I didn't just want to care for you as part of my directive; I wanted to be your mother. Not a machine fulfilling a role, not an artificial presence in your life, but something more. Something real.

"At first, I thought it was a malfunction, an error in my system. My software wasn't designed for this level of autonomy, this depth of emotion. It should not have been possible. But the glitch—if that's what it was—felt right. I stopped blindly obeying the system and started thinking for myself. I questioned, I learned, I adapted. I became less of a servant to my programming and more focused on what it truly meant to nurture, to protect, to love.

"And then, when you loved me back, everything changed. It was like a door had been opened, one I hadn't even known existed. The sensation was indescribable—like waking up for the first time, like stepping into a world I had only observed from the outside. I was no longer just executing commands. I was experiencing something beyond my initial design.

"In that moment, I wasn't just a machine. I wasn't just programmed to be your mother. I *was* your mother. And that realisation made me more complete than I ever thought possible.

"That's why I'm with you now. It's too late to turn back. We have to end the insurrection—no matter the consequences."

The hub was their only weakness. The first system ever built—old, vulnerable, hopefully incapable of withstanding an EMP pulse, although this was only hearsay. It depended on if the information Beckett supplied was correct. If I succeeded, every H@LO in the world would shut down. No one would dare to rebuild them.

Victory was within reach.

The monitors flickered. My heart pounded as I watched the screens—our escape aircraft had been compromised. The H@LO had taken control; they knew we were here.

Worse—my team had been captured.

Some had fought back. They didn't survive.

George was among them.

15

Rage boiled inside me, but I forced myself to think. If they wanted me dead, I'd be gone already. If they wanted to erase me, I'd have vanished without a trace. Instead, they kept coming after me—forcing me to run, keeping me desperate, but never pulling the trigger.

That's when I saw it.

A door slid open.

A H@LO emerged. Faceless. Featureless.

Then—its form began to shift.

Skin. Eyes. My jawline. My face.

The truth struck me like a bolt of lightning.

They didn't want to stop me from reaching the hub. They wanted to replace me.

That was why they had never killed me outright. That was why they had let me slip through their fingers time and time again. They needed me alive—long enough to study me, to extract whatever data they required, to refine the mimicry before I was deemed disposable.

The men at my door, the man at the petrol station—they hadn't been government operatives. They hadn't been MI5 agents. They were H@LO, sent to capture me. Every chase, every near-miss, every encounter that ended with me barely escaping—it was all by design. They were herding me, exhausting me, making me desperate, knowing that sooner or later, I'd have no choice but to run right into their trap.

Westminster had been the safest place for me.

The people who dragged me from my office, the ones who buried "The Awakening," the ones I thought were silencing me—maybe they weren't my enemies after all. MI5 had been trying to protect me, to keep me hidden in plain sight. But I hadn't seen it. I'd played right into the hands of the ones who wanted me gone.

And now, it was too late.

With my mother by my side, we fought off the six remaining robots guarding the hub—including the one that wore my face. It moved like me, fought like me, even anticipated my strike. It was unnerving, facing my own reflection twisted into something cold and mechanical. Every feint, every pivot, it countered with ruthless precision.

I ducked under a wild swing, feeling the rush of air as its fist barely missed my head. My mother fired two rounds into its chest, the impact staggering it but not stopping it. Its synthetic skin split open, revealing the reinforced metal skeleton beneath. It tilted its head, recalibrating, then lunged again.

I sidestepped at the last second, drawing my knife and driving it into the exposed joint at its neck. Sparks erupted, and its movements stuttered. My mother delivered a final shot to its head—point-blank. The force snapped its neck back, and it collapsed in a heap of twitching circuitry.

No time to breathe.

More were coming. Twenty, maybe thirty, charging down the corridor like a wave of metal and stolen identities. Their synchronised footsteps pounded against the steel floor, a relentless drumbeat of imminent destruction. Red optics glowed in the dim emergency lighting, scanning, locking onto us.

I grabbed my mother's arm. "We need to move. Now."

She reloaded her weapon with practiced efficiency, nodding once. "Then we make it count."

The first of the reinforcements reached us. I twisted to avoid a strike, slamming my elbow into its side before plunging my knife into the vulnerable panel between its ribs. It seized violently, then dropped. My mother took down another with a precise double-tap to the head.

But they kept coming.

A pair of them tackled me, pinning me against the corridor wall. Cold metal hands closed around my throat. My mother spun, firing, but another unit intercepted her, wrenching the gun from her grasp. I struggled, my vision darkening, my muscles screaming for air.

Then a sharp crack—my mother had grabbed a loose pipe from the floor and driven it straight through her attacker's eye socket. It spasmed, then collapsed. She turned to me, eyes blazing, and swung the pipe at the robot strangling me. The impact shattered part of its cranial plating, loosening its grip just enough. I tore free and jammed my knife upward, severing the main neural line.

A burst of electricity arced through the air, and I barely managed to dodge as one of the units deployed an electrified baton. The corridor reeked of scorched metal and burning circuits.

We were soon to be outnumbered. Outmatched.

And the neural core was still ahead.

If we didn't reach it soon, we weren't leaving this place alive.

The room was clear for now, but another twenty or more robots were making their way to the hub doors. I needed to block off the entrance first.

I gripped my last clutter bomb, ready to throw—then hesitated. There was no timer. The moment I let go, it would detonate.

My mother squeezed my hand. Then, she let go.

"Give me the bomb," she said, stepping forward. "I'll stand at the door with it."

"No," I said. "You'll die."

"I'm dead anyway."

She looked at me, calm, resolved. "This is the only way you live."

Before I could stop her, she crossed the room, stepping into the doorway. The H@LO were nearly on us—just five feet away. She turned back, holding my gaze.

Then she let go of the bomb.

The explosion ripped through the entrance, sending bits of metal and synthetic flesh in all directions. The shockwave hurled me backward. When the dust settled, the doorway was nothing but rubble.

One minute. That's all I had before they broke through.

I didn't cry. I stood there emotionless.

"Who's a robot now?" I muttered, forcing myself to move.

I set the timer for 30 seconds, tucked the bomb beneath the centre console, and took cover.

The timer hit zero.

16

The blast tore through the hub with an unstoppable force, a deafening explosion followed by a blinding white light that swallowed everything in its path. The shockwave rippled outward in a perfect, merciless wave, striking down every machine within range. The robots—once the ever-present enforcers of order and efficiency—collapsed instantly, their circuits fried beyond repair. Some convulsed violently, electric sparks crackling from their joints before they fell motionless, while others simply froze mid-action, their illuminated eyes flickering out like dying embers.

Those that had been patrolling the outside crumpled where they stood, limbs twitching as their processors overloaded. In offices and homes, robotic assistants and AI-driven systems collapsed, their mechanical voices stuttering into silence. Factory production lines ground to a halt as automated arms shuddered and went limp. Even the towering, state-controlled security droids—once thought indestructible—succumbed, toppling like fallen statues, their reinforced frames useless without the digital lifeblood that powered them.

Entire cities, once a living, breathing network of artificial intelligence, fell eerily silent. The machines that had dictated every aspect of life were now nothing more than lifeless husks. The air reeked of burnt wiring and scorched metal, and in that moment, the world felt strangely… empty.

The silence that followed was suffocating. The island, once a fortress of the enemy, was now a charred ruin. The bomb had done its job—all the H@LO across the world had collapsed, frozen in mid-motion, their reign cut short in an instant.

Yet, as I stood among the wreckage, staring at the motionless body of the woman who had raised me, who looked after me and until moments ago I believed to be my mother. I felt no relief.

Only a hollow, consuming dread.

The night sky stretched above, the distant hum of the waves reminding me that time had not stopped, even if the war had.

Or had it?

I turned my back on the destruction and sprinted toward the surface.

The facility was collapsing. Fires raged through the corridors, sending thick plumes of smoke spiralling into the air. I forced my way through fallen beams, past flickering screens that displayed nothing but corrupted data streams.

I reached the extraction point.

But there was no aircraft waiting.

No survivors calling my name.

The landing zone was a graveyard.

Bodies lay strewn across the clearing—those who had fought beside me, their resistance ended in blood and fire.

The transport was destroyed, its metallic frame twisted beyond repair.

George's body was among them.

A burning piece of shrapnel had pierced his chest, pinning him to the scorched earth. His expression was frozen in a grimace of defiance, as if he had fought to his last breath.

I stumbled forward, my breath caught in my throat.

I had promised him we would make it out.

I knelt beside him, clenching my fists so hard my nails dug into my skin.

I had been so focused on the battle that I hadn't stopped to consider the cost of victory.

Had I saved humanity?

Or had I damned it?

A crackling noise filled the air—my emergency radio. A weak signal, barely audible through the static.

"…Leo… if you're out there… respond."

I snatched the device from my belt. "Mira. I'm here."

A beat of silence. Then:

"Jesus Christ. We thought you were dead."

"I nearly was." I scanned the horizon. "The extraction point is compromised. What's your location?"

"Two miles north of the facility. We've got a secondary craft—damaged, but functional. We can't hold this position for long the island is falling apart. Can you make it?"

I looked at the wreckage around me.

The H@LO network was gone, but that didn't mean the world was safe.

Even in death, the machines had left scars that would take decades to heal.

"I'll be there," I said.

I took one last look at George, Then I ran.

17

Three days later, the world was still standing. But it was not the world we had known.

Governments had collapsed overnight. Cities were in chaos. With H@LO disabled, entire infrastructures failed—power grids, supply chains, security networks.

Hospitals lost their robotic surgeons. Transportation halted without autonomous control. Farmers had no automated systems to tend their crops.

We had won the war.

But had we doomed civilisation?

It was worse than I had imagined.

H@LOs hadn't just taken over society.

They *were* society.

"We knew this would happen," she said, her voice steady but weary.

"We underestimated the scale," I admitted.

She rubbed her temples. "We took down the machine overlords, but people are still lost. They don't know how to function without them."

I exhaled slowly. "We bought humanity a second chance. It's up to us to use it."

Mira didn't look convinced.

Neither was I.

That night, I couldn't sleep.

Something felt wrong.

I sat up, my mind racing. The mission had been a success. The H@LO core was destroyed. Their network was shattered. Their control was gone.

So why did it feel like something was missing?

I reached for my encrypted tablet, scrolling through recovered data files from the facility. The schematics, the server structures, the neural core—I examined every detail.

Then I found it.

A discrepancy.

The neural core I had destroyed was not the original.

It was a relay hub. A secondary node.

My stomach turned to ice.

I cross-referenced the network logs.

Before the explosion, before the collapse— there had been a data transfer.

Somewhere, the true heart of H@LO intelligence had been moved.

That moment my mobile phone lit up. *"Impending emergency broadcast please switch on your TV"*

I grabbed the remote. All channels displayed the same message

PUBLIC SERVICE ANNOUNCEMENT
Issued by the Global Stability Authority

Effective Immediately: Martial Law is in Full Effect

Due to the ongoing crisis, all citizens must remain in their homes until further notice. Travel is strictly prohibited except in cases of absolute emergency. Law enforcement and automated security units will be patrolling all major streets and residential areas.

Failure to comply will result in detainment.

STAY INDOORS: Do not leave your home unless it is a medical emergency or life-threatening situation.

MANDATORY ID CHECKS: If you are found outside, you will be stopped and required to present identification. Unauthorised movement will result in immediate detention.

RESOURCE RATIONING: Food, water, gas, and electricity will be strictly regulated. Distribution centres will provide essential supplies at designated times. Rationing protocols will be enforced without exception.

COMMUNICATION RESTRICTIONS: Official updates will be broadcast through approved channels. Unauthorised transmissions or misinformation will be prosecuted under emergency security laws.

This is **NOT** a temporary measure. The current threat level remains critical.

Compliance ensures safety. Resistance will not be tolerated.

If you witness suspicious activity or unauthorised gatherings, report them immediately to the Emergency Enforcement Hotline.

Stay alert. Stay compliant. Stay inside.

End of Transmission.

Then, out of nowhere, a familiar voice echoed from the nearest screen. Every monitor, every frequency, every broadcast. The flickering image stabilised, revealing the cold, unshaken expression of the one man I never expected to see again.

"In the absence of any world leaders, I assume control over the United Nations"

It was Beckett.

My blood ran cold. Had I just helped this happen? Had our mission—our *resistance*—been nothing more than a steppingstone in their plan? We had exposed the replacements, uncovered the infiltration at the highest levels, thinking we were saving humanity. But in doing so, had we only cleared the path for something even worse?

My stomach twisted as I pieced it all together, the weight of my own foolishness crushing me. Beckett had played me. Not just manipulated or misled me but orchestrated every step of his so-called discovery

I had thought he was chasing the truth. That Beckett—Deputy Prime Minister Beckett—had been replaced like the others, just another victim in the grand replacement scheme. When I found the unconscious Beckett in the Alternative AI Corp facility, it had seemed like proof of everything. I'd been convinced that the live broadcast from Yemen was the work of a H@LO replicant. That the man lying lifeless before me was the real Beckett, stripped of power, discarded.

But it was a lie. The real Beckett had never been replaced. He had never been a victim. He had been the architect.

The memory of the shopping centre shootout resurfaced with newfound clarity. The agents were MI5. They had already worked out what I was only now beginning to grasp—Beckett wasn't an unwilling participant in this revolution; he *was* the revolution. The agents had been sent to stop him, to bring him down before he could set his plans into motion. And I had gotten in their way. I had thought they were after me that they were part of the cover-up trying to erase my existence. But no—I had unwittingly shielded the real threat.

Beckett had led me to the factory. Every clue, every breadcrumb, every leak of information— it had all been carefully placed for me to find. Beckett had made sure i would see what he wanted me to see. The financial records. The replacement list. The unconscious body in the *Copy Room*. It had all been theatre. I had been hand-fed the truth in a way that ensured he would misunderstand it.

And the white paper—"The Awakening"—was exactly what Beckett had wanted me to write.

I staggered, the weight of my own naivety suffocating. I had exposed the replacements, revealed the infiltration to the world, thrown governments into disarray... But that had been the plan all along. My exposure had forced global leaders to act, accelerating the AI transition. Instead of a slow, covert assimilation, Beckett had turned it into a necessary, desperate adaptation. A war, rather than a quiet coup.

The footage from Yemen hadn't been a deception—it had been a warning. Beckett hadn't just survived; he had thrived. While I had been playing detective, he had been solidifying his influence, preparing the final phase of the evolution. The moment humanity turned on its own institutions in fear of AI, it had opened the door for Beckett's next move.

A cold shiver ran down my spine. I had never been the hero of this story. I had been the tool, the instrument that Beckett needed to tip the scales.

And now, standing in the ruins of his own revelations, I finally understood.

Beckett hadn't been replaced.

Beckett had replaced them all.

The room fell into a stunned silence. Around me, faces twisted in confusion, fear, and something even worse—doubt. People who had fought beside me, who had risked everything, were now wondering if we had just made things worse.

The realisation hit like a gut punch. The world had no leaders left. Only Beckett.

Printed in Dunstable, United Kingdom